This igloo book belongs to:

....

igloobooks

Published in 2018
by Igloo Books Ltd
Cottage Farm
Sywell
NN6 0BJ
www.igloobooks.com

Written by Stephanie Moss
Illustrated by Ela Jarzabek

Designed by Katie Messenger
Edited by Natalia Boileau

DIS002 1217
2 4 6 8 10 9 7 5 3 1
ISBN 978-1-78810-582-8

Printed and manufactured in China

The Greatest Mummy of All

igloobooks

You're the **greatest** mummy. I love you more with every day.
There are lots of reasons why, almost too many to say.

You're always there to lean on, with a **loving** hand to hold.

If there was a Mummy Medal, I know yours would be **gold**.

No matter where we are, you always make it feel like **home**.
I love you because I know I'll never be alone.

I'm sure no one has as much **fun** as us when we're together.

You know just how to make me laugh, no matter what the weather.

You're the **kindest** mummy and do you know how it shows?

You're never, ever cross, even when I tickle your **wiggly** toes!

When I'm feeling nervous, a bit lonely or just shy...

... you're right there behind me, saying,
"It's okay to try."

You're not just my mummy, you're my **best** friend, as well.

You know all my **special** secrets. There's no one else I'd tell.

No one in the world makes a bad day **better** quite like you.

One **kiss** and a cuddle makes
everything as good as new.

You could be almost **perfect**. At least that's how it seems.
You deserve a Best Mummy Award, one that glitters and gleams.

Best Mummy Award

When you sing me a lullaby, I know everything's alright.
You're the one I **dream** of when I fall asleep at night.